this

little 🌳 ORCHARD

book belongs to

....
..... 12

....

ORCHARD BOOKS
96 Leonard Street, London EC2A 4XD
Orchard Books Australia
14 Mars Road, Lane Cove, NSW 2066
1 84121 381 0 (hardback)
1 84121 387 X (paperback)
First published in Great Britain in 2000
Text © Sally Grindley 2000
Illustrations © Andy Ellis 2000
The rights of Sally Grindley and Andy Ellis to be identified
as the author and illustrator respectively of this work have been asserted by
them in accordance with the Copyright, Designs and Patents Act, 1988.
A CIP catalogue record for this book is available from the British Library.
2 4 6 8 10 9 7 5 3 1
Printed in Italy

Eat up, Piglittle

Sally Grindley • Andy Ellis

little ORCHARD

It was Piglittle's dinnertime.

"Eat up your sprouts, my little sugarplum," said Primrose Pig.

"Don't like them," said Piglittle. "They're horrid."

"Well try some potato, poppet," said Primrose Pig.

"Don't want it," said Piglittle and ran out into the yard.

"I don't know what to do with my youngest one," said Primrose Pig to Gertie Goat. "He's so good, but he won't eat his food."

"He'll eat when he's hungry," said Gertie Goat.

Piglittle ran round and round the farmyard.

Soon he began to feel very hungry.

He went to the henhouse.
"What are you eating, Hetty?"
he asked.

"Some lovely corn," said Hetty Hen.
"Try some."

Piglittle tried some. "Yuck!" he said.
"It's horrid."

He went to the pond.
"What are you eating, Dabble?"
he asked.

"Some lovely weed," said Dabble Duck. "Try some."

Piglittle tried some. "Yuck!" he said. "It's horrid."

He went and found Gertie Goat.
"What are you eating, Gertie?"
he asked.

"Some lovely green shoots," said
Gertie Goat. "Try some."

Piglittle tried some. "Yuck!" he said.
"They're horrid."

He went to the stable.
"What are you eating, Henry?"
he asked.

"Some lovely hay," said Henry Horse. "Try some."

Piglittle tried some. "Yuck!" he said. "It's horrid."

By now Piglittle was feeling *very* hungry indeed.

"I've made you something delicious," called Primrose Pig. "A treat for little piglets."

Piglittle ran over and tried a tiny bit. . .and then a little bit more.

"What is it?" he asked.

"Sprout and potato mash," said Primrose Pig.

"Mmm, it's lovely!" said Piglittle.